Mac & Cheese, Pleeeeze!

by Eleanor May
illustrated by Diane Palmisciano

Kane Press
New York

For all the kids of SLV, especially the kids whose names didn't get in the story—E.M.

Text copyright © 2008 by Eleanor May
Illustrations copyright © 2008 by Diane Palmisciano

Library of Congress Cataloging-in-Publication Data

May, Eleanor.
  Mac & cheese, pleeeeze! / by Eleanor May ; illustrated by Diane Palmisciano.
    p. cm. — (Math matters)
  "Mental Math-Grades: 1/3."
  Summary: While campaigning for her favorite meal—macaroni and cheese—in the school's first ever "Lunch Election," Caitlin tallies the committed votes in her head.
  ISBN-13: 978-1-57565-260-3 (alk. paper)
  [1. Food—Fiction. 2. Elections—Fiction. 3. Counting—Fiction. 4. Schools—Fiction.]
  I. Palmisciano, Diane, ill. II. Title. III. Title: Mac and cheese, pleeeeze! IV. Title: Mac & cheese, please!
  PZ7.M4513Mac 2008
  [E]—dc22
                              2007026568

eISBN: 978-1-57565-581-9

10 9 8 7 6 5 4 3

First published in the United States of America in 2008 by Kane Press, Inc.
3–CG–12/1/2016

Math Matters is a registered trademark of Kane Press, Inc.

Book Design: Edward Miller

Visit us online at **www.kanepress.com**

 Like us on Facebook
facebook.com/kanepress

 Follow us on Twitter
@kanepress

I like my teacher, Mr. Moore. I really do.
But he comes up with the weirdest ideas.

"A *lunch food* election?" I roll my eyes.
"Mayor Meatloaf? President Pizza?"

My best friend, Luna, laughs. "Oh, come
on, Caitlin. I think it sounds like fun."

"Class," Mr. Moore said this morning. "We are running the Spring Fest Lunch Election!"

"Huh?" we all asked.

He explained. "You'll each pick a lunch you'd like to eat at Spring Fest. Then you try to get other students to vote for your choice. The whole school will be voting—so good luck, and may the best lunch win!"

"It'll be a disaster," I tell Luna after school. "Remember last month's science project?"

Sure, we all liked the worm farm—until Sam and Joey got into a scuffle, knocked the worms over, and made a dirty, squirmy mess.

"That was gross," Luna admits. "But this is *lunch*. No dirt, no worms. At least, I hope not!"

Luna and I stop and take a look at Mr. Moore's election rules.

ELECTION RULES FOR
MR. MOORE'S CLASS

• Choose one lunch from the cafeteria menu.
• Try to get other kids in the school to vote for your lunch.
• The winning lunch will be served at Spring Fest!

"What's the point?" I grumble. "Everyone will vote for Peppy Pizza."

"Not me," Luna says. "I'm voting for my favorite—Tofu Surprise."

Sometimes Luna is as weird as Mr. Moore.

I forget about the election until the next day on the bus.

"Check out my campaign posters for Tuna Melt," Annie says.

I raise an eyebrow. "You made posters?"

She unrolls one to show me her slogan.

Sam snorts. "You haven't got a chance. Wait till you hear my Broccoli Stuffed Potato speech."

I shake my head. "I can't believe you two even care who wins this goofy election."

"Don't *you?*" Annie asks.

"Yeah, right," I say. "Broccoli battles tuna. Big thrill!"

At school I check out the sign-up sheet. I guess I have to pick something.

Wait—nobody has signed up for Mac & Cheese? That's crazy! It's the best thing on the menu! I put down my name.

"Not bad," Annie says. "Of course, it's not as good as Tuna Melt."

**SPRING FEST LUNCH ELECTION
SIGN UP NOW!**

PEPPY PIZZA	Joey
BROCCOLI STUFFED POTATO	SAM
BEAN BURRITOS	Mia
TUNA MELT	Annie
MAC & CHEESE	Caitlin
FUNKY CHICKEN	Hank
TOFU SURPRISE	Luna
EY W	Kelan

At lunch I scarf down Mac & Cheese while Luna counts the votes she has lined up. "My brother and his chess club friends promised to vote for Tofu Surprise," she tells me.

"Really? That's their favorite lunch?"

Luna turns pink. "My brother said he'd bring in donuts if they voted for Tofu."

Joey looks up from his notebook.

"Counting your votes for Pizza?" I ask him.

"Nope," he says. "For *all* the lunches. See? Peppy Pizza is on top so far. Number 2 is . . ."

I stop eating. "Broccoli Stuffed Potato?"

"Sam's been making lots of speeches," says Joey.

"Where's Mac & Cheese?" I ask Joey.

He shows me. "Down at the bottom."

I can't believe it. Mac & Cheese is doing worse than Turkey Wieners?

This could be embarrassing. I'd better get some votes!

I find my sister, Sophie, on the swings.
"What lunch are you voting for?" I ask.
  "Pizza," she says.
  "But I need votes for Mac & Cheese."
Sophie smiles. "Okay."
  "Okay, you'll vote for Mac & Cheese?"
  "No. I like Pizza."

Sophie's friend Rachel says, "I'll vote for Mac & Cheese if you'll push me."

Now I can count on two votes—Rachel's and mine. But if I have to get all my votes this way, my arms are going to fall off!

1 + 1 is a simple fact. You don't need pencil and paper. You can do math in your head! That's called **mental math**.

I spot my neighbor Charlie on the slide. "Will you vote for Mac & Cheese?" I ask.

"Sam wants me to vote for Broccoli Stuffed Potato," he tells me.

I'm about to walk off. Then he says, "But you're my neighbor. And broccoli is gross."

Three votes. Well, it's a start. Still, I need more if I don't want to look like a total loser.

Who else can I get to vote for Mac & Cheese? I can't ask anyone in my class. They're all voting for their own lunches.

I could try Charlie's brother, Nick. He's my neighbor, too, even if he is only in kindergarten.

"Nick, do you like Mac & Cheese?" I ask.

"I just ate," he says. "I'm not hungry."

"What about when you *are* hungry?"

"But I'm not."

I finally talk all the little kids into voting for Mac & Cheese—except Nick. He says he's still not hungry.

Four more votes!

During math I try to think up a slogan. Luna leans over. "I thought you didn't *care* about the lunch election?"

"I don't," I say, and cover up my notes. Me and my big mouth. Now I wish I hadn't teased the other kids for trying to get votes.

The next day some fifth grade girls see me putting up posters. "Cute!" one of them says. "You've got my vote. I love Mac & Cheese!"

Her friends say, "Me, too."

Great! Three more votes. I'm up to ten. And I'm starting to like this election!

I wish I could add everything up on paper, like Luna. But if anyone saw me, they'd know how much I want the votes. I'd never live it down!

Sam is putting up posters, too.
I read them and laugh.

Then I see another poster.

Hmmph. That's not very funny.

Two kids from the soccer team are looking at my poster. I edge closer. "I like Peppy Pizza better," one of them is saying.

The girl says, "Yeah, but the Frisbee team is voting for Pizza. We can't do what they do."

"No way," the boy agrees. "The soccer team vote goes to Mac & Cheese."

Wow! That's twenty kids!

When you start to add greater numbers, you can use special thinking strategies. I know 1 + 2 = 3, so 10 + 20 = 30.

In class, Luna looks bummed. "They took Tofu Surprise off the menu. The cooks said it wasn't popular enough. Can you believe it?"

Actually, I can. But all I do is shrug.

"Now the chess club can't vote for it." Luna gives me a look. "Too bad you don't care who wins. We could all switch to Mac & Cheese."

I check to make sure no one else can hear me. "Maybe I do care—a little," I admit.

Luna smiles. "Well, in that case . . ."

There are 28 kids in the chess club, and Luna makes 29. Twenty-nine more votes!

Best friends are the best.

At choir practice I whisper to the girl next to me. *"Choir kids stick together. Vote for Mac & Cheese. Pass it on."*

The news travels fast. Everyone nods and smiles. *Yes!* Thirteen more votes.

⚡ **THINK** ⚡
59 and 10 is 69, and 3 more makes 72.

I run into Charlie on my way home.

"Guess what?" he says. "I got my whole class to vote for Mac & Cheese tomorrow. All but Timmy. His sister Annie says he has to vote for Tuna Melt."

That's another 31 votes! Awesome!

72 + 31 = 103

⟿ THINK ⟿
I know that 72 + 30 = 102,
and 1 more makes 103.

NAME	VOTES
Pizza	104
Potato	104
Mac & Cheese	103

At recess the next day, Joey comes over. "You're not at the bottom anymore!"

"Oh?" I try not to sound too interested. "So now I'm ahead of Turkey Wieners?"

"Even better," he says. "Pizza and Potato are tied for first, and Mac & Cheese is next!"

Wow! I'm just a vote behind Joey and Sam!

Back in class Annie rushes up to me.

"Did you hear?" she says. "Sam and Joey got in a big fight over Sam's PIZZA IS FOR PIZZA FACES poster. Now Mr. Moore won't let either of them vote!"

One vote less for Pizza. One vote less for Stuffed Potato. *Woo-hoo!* It's a three-way tie!

Now, if I can just get one more vote . . .

"Sophie, you're my *sister*," I say. "Can't you vote for Mac & Cheese?"

She plants her shovel in the sand. "PIZZA."

So much for sisters.

Then Nick looks at me. "I'm hungry," he says. "I want Mac & Cheese."

That means . . .

"Say Cheese!" I yell. "Mac & Cheese, The Lunch You Love!"

I jump up and down. Luna gives me a high five.

Annie stares. "I thought you said it was a goofy election."

"Totally goofy," I say. "Totally weird. And I sure hope I win!"

THE VOTES ARE IN!

WINNER: Mac & Cheese ———————— 104 votes

2nd Place < Broccoli Stuffed Potato ———————— 103 votes

Peppy Pizza ———————— 103 votes

MENTAL MATH CHART

Put your pencil down! Get ready to **ADD IN YOUR HEAD!**
Look at what each kid below is thinking.
Then find the answer.
The first problem is done for you.

1. Find 6 + 8.

I know **8** is 2 more than **6**.

Think: **6** + **6** is a doubles fact.
6 plus **6** is **12**.

So: **12** plus **2** more is **14**.

---

2. Find 48 + 15.

Think: You can "break up"
numbers to make adding easier!

I know 15 is 10 plus 5.

$$\textbf{48} \quad + \quad 10 \quad + \quad 5$$
$$58 \quad + \quad 5$$
$$?$$

So: **48** + **15** = ?

Answers: 58 + 5 = 63,
so, 48 + 15 = 63

---

3. Find 24 + 81.

Think: A two-digit number is made
of some tens and some ones.

I can add
the **tens** and then
add the **ones!**

$$24 \quad = \quad \textbf{20} \quad + \quad 4$$
$$+\ 81 \quad = \quad \textbf{80} \quad + \quad 1$$
$$100 \quad + \quad 5 \quad = \quad ?$$

So: **24** + **81** = ?

Answers: 100 + 5 = 105,
so, 24 + 81 = 105